PIG

and the
Ice-cream
Cake

Barbara Catchpole

Illustrated by metaphrog

Ransom

Good to see you!

Ho-ly mo-ly! I remember you! You've grown!
Have you been standing with your feet in cow
poo?

My mum says
that makes you
grow! Or maybe
that's plants ...

Cows are quite big, so perhaps it works for
everything.

Anyway, it's great to see you! I've grown a
centimetre since the last book! Mum marks it
on the shed wall.

What have you been up to since I saw you last? Don't worry – you'll probably get away with it. Just don't let your mum search your room, or she'll find it.

Mine does my bedroom all the time. She says it's 'because she loves me' – but I think she's just plain nosy.

I always know she's done it because she leaves marks in the dust. She throws away the old food from under the bed. I have to hide all my good stuff round Raj's.

Raj's mum trusts 'her little man'. I'll say it again – she's got no idea how to bring up boys.

She trusts him. Ha ha!

Under Raj's bed I've still
got some fart bombs
from when my dad took
me to the joke shop. I'm
saving them for the last
day of term assembly.

That should keep it good and short.

Fart bombs are much better than just farting.
Less effort, and you can get the smell a bit
away from you before the teachers notice it.

And anyway, sometimes you just don't have a
fart in you.

So how are your family? Let me tell you what's been going on with my nutters, then you can tell me about yours!

Gran

Gran and Santa are still going out. Every little bit of their bodies is falling apart. Some bits even drop off.

They always go to the doctor's together (quite often!) and it keeps them happy.

Here is Gran's timetable for next week. It is under a magnet on our freezer, because she is always round here drinking our tea and eating

8

our biscuits. So her timetable might as well be round here too.

Monday:

Look after Vampire Baby. Leave teeth at dentists. Buy soup.

Tuesday:

~~Optishun. Optyshun~~ Eye test. Bingo. Clip toenails.

Wednesday:

Pick up teeth.

~~Karyochy carryokie~~ Sing-song down the Slug and Lettuce.

Thursday:

Going round Fred's for a curry – try out
new teeth.

Friday:

Having me hair and
me corns done. Fred's
Ear Hair Trim Day.

Saturday:

Going to Las Vegas with Johnny Depp.
Take reading glasses and new teeth.

Sunday:

Tesco's.

Beetle drive at St Wilf's.

Notes

1. The Slug and Lettuce is the pub by the betting shop. It used to be the Dog and Ferret, but then it needed a new sign and the bloke did it cheap. But he couldn't do dogs or ferrets. It's quite a good slug.

2. St Wilfred's is the Day Centre on the corner. Gran is Head Wrinkly there.

I am scared to go in. You can get stuck between wheelchairs, scooter things and walking frames, and then you can't get out for hours. It's no good shouting for help because everybody shouts, and so nobody notices you. They're all deaf anyway.

In the Day Centre nobody can hear you scream.

3. Santa is called Fred. You'd think he'd be called Noel or Nick, wouldn't you?

4. Beetle drives aren't as much fun as they sound. I went to one once, thinking there might be giant beetles. There aren't.

5. Gran can't spell.

6. I don't think Gran even knows Johnny Depp, but she might – you can't tell. You can't believe a word she says – she's like the weather girl on telly.

Suki

Big, big news! Huge, ginormous news!

Suki has decided to be a Supermod-el and earn
loads of money and buy us a big house.

She has two huge false eyelashes that she
actually sticks onto
her eyelids with
special stuff.

She leaves them
next to the sink at night. They look like insects
with hundreds of legs.

It's totally gross.

(Eat your heart out, English teacher! We're doing similes this week and I rock like a ... like a ... well, like a big rocky thing.)

We only have one toilet in our house. It's a real pain when Suki's in the bath. Sometimes she's in there for days. She lights candles and has music and smelly stick things.

She says I stink up the bathroom, but she makes it smell a lot more and she puts slippy stuff in the bath. You could break your neck in there!

She *says* she reads a book in the bath. Sometimes she's in there so long I think she's writing a book. It makes me really mad, especially if I've been playing a computer game and I've left it until the last minute.

I have to shout:

'Muuuuuummmm

mmmmmmmm

mmmmmmmmm!'

over and over again

really loud. Which isn't easy when you want a wee.

Then Mum makes Suki get out
and wait on the landing in a
towel.

I'm not sure about the
supermodel thing, but I think
Suki might be turning into
some kind of fish. Or a
barnacle.

When she buys us a big house, I hope it has two
loos.

Mum

Mum's met a bloke at pottery. He's the bloke

who teaches people how to make the ugliest pots on the planet (probably in the whole universe, if aliens make pots).

His name is Bob and he's always around ours. Bob, bob, bobbing about. He makes me angry and I hate him.

Fifi Ulrika Trixiebelle the Fifth and Princess Kate

I've had a great time at Tiffany's. Her hamster died and we buried it in her back garden, next to the dustbin.

Fifi Ulrika Trixiebelle the Fifth was lying in its bed with its little paws in the air and a breadstick in its mouth, when Tiffany noticed it wasn't moving.

FUT (I called it FUT for short) was just a huge ball of fluff. You couldn't even tell which end was which until it moved.

Tiffany's mum (who is Governor at our school, whatever that is) said:

'It's gone to the Great Hamster Cage in the sky.'

Tiffany was a bit upset. But hamsters don't live five minutes, so what do you expect?

BIN

We made cross of lolly sticks. I enjoyed the singing and I got to eat two lollies, one after the other.

Tiff's mum has to keep throwing things at their cat to stop it digging FUT back up.

Tiffany says she's going to get another hamster. She's going to call it 'Kate', after the princess. So that's OK.

Tuesday

When I was twelve I was really excited about my birthday party, but it didn't happen because it was the day Dad moved out.

Mum said she couldn't do a party because she had too many things to think about. Grown-ups! Dead selfish!

Anyway, last week we were going round Tesco's and I was looking at all the birthday cakes. I didn't cry, but I got a bit of something in my eye - well, in both of them. I was just rubbing them a bit.

Mum went quiet and she thought for a bit and then she said:

'Hey, don't cry! I tell you what - would you like a birthday party now, Pig?'

'Can I have a cake?'

'Yeah.'

'And candles?'

'Yeah.'

'But it's not my birthday any more!'

I wasn't crying – I had hiccoughs all of a sudden.

'Yeah, but we won't tell them that, or you won't get any presents! Come on, let's do it!'

So I had my late, late, birthday party in the downstairs bit of the Osmans' burger bar. Osman Osman is in my class and we got it cheap.

It was on a Saturday and I had invited all my mates from school. Mum spent the whole week baking a big chocolate birthday cake. It was going to have twelve candles and everything.

The best bit was on the Tuesday when my dad phoned from Spain.

I told him all about it and I said:

'Will you come to my party, Dad?'

He's great at parties. He does this thing sticking straws up his nose and rushing around being a monster.

I don't miss him. Really I don't. I just thought it would be good if he came.

Just between you and me, I thought maybe he and Mum would get back together and maybe he would stay and we might move to the seaside.

I could have new trainers.

Maybe.

Like in the films.

It could happen.

It went all quiet at the other end and then he

said:

'Yes, of course, Pig. I'll be there. Try to

keep me away!'

I told Mum and her mouth went all funny, until it looked like a cat's bum.

You know how you can see cat's bums when they put their tails straight up, like they are bumper cars? (I'm pretty sure that's a simile.) I just want to make it plain I don't go around lifting up cats' tails to look at their bums.

Then Mum said 'huh' and her eyes went all narrow.

Raj

When I asked Raj to my birthday party, he said:

'I didn't think it was your birthday, Pig.'

I told him the whole thing. He won't tell anyone. He's my mate.

Wednesday

Dad didn't come on Wednesday.

I thought he was probably buying a plane

ticket. I told everyone at school he was coming over just for my birthday party.

I said it was my birthday, so they should bring a present. I told them my dad would bring a brilliant present.

When I told Raj, his mum was listening. She narrowed her eyes as well, and her mouth did the cat's bum thing.

She shook her head a bit, as if she had water in her ears, and her earrings jangled.

Thursday

Dad would probably come at the very last minute and then stay on for a while.

I asked Gran if he could stay with her. Her mouth was already wrinkly so it was hard to tell about the bum thing, but her eyes did go all narrow.

She said she would really love to go to a noisy,

shouty, messy children's birthday party, but – it was a shame – she was 'hitting Vegas with Johnny'.

She said it wasn't even my birthday, but:

> 'Here – have a fiver!'

Result!

Friday

I spent the evening sitting on the windowsill in the Room We Never Use, looking down our street.

Mum wanted me to go to bed, so she phoned

Dad on his mobile.
He didn't answer
it.

I told her not to
bother. It was
going to be alright!
He was on the
plane and that
was why he couldn't
answer his mobile.

Saturday —
happy unbirthday to me!

Mum had finished my cake. It was huge and

chocolatey and drippy and sat on the kitchen

table next to Harry in his cage.

It was driving Harry crazy. He could see it, but

he couldn't get to it.

Harry was trying to eat the whole cage so that

he could get out and eat the whole cake. He had

already eaten a bit of Mum's thumb.

It was five to three - time to leave for my

unbirthday party.

'Let's go!' Mum said.

'We can't go yet. Dad's not here!'

Mum put her arm round me.

'I don't think he's coming, Pig.'

'Get off me! He is! He said he would!'

"He said he would be rich and we'd live at the seaside. He's a bit of a liar, Pig. He just can't help it. Don't be upset! Look, you've got a lovely cake and Bob's coming,' she said.

'But he's not my dad, is he? HE'S – NOT – MY – DAD!'

I was shouting at Mum now.

I pushed her off me and then my hands shot out and I knocked the cake right off the table onto the kitchen floor.

It splatted everywhere.

Mum had spent ages making it. She sort of went 'oofff' and sat down suddenly.

Then she went bright red and started shouting at me:

'That's it, young man! No party for you!'

Bob and my mum's name

It was Bob who saved me.

    'It's not the kid's fault, Susan,' he said.

I don't know why Bob thinks Mum's called
Susan. That's just weird!

My mum's real names are Siouxie Kiaora.
'Siouxie' is because her dad
liked a singer called Siouxie,
and 'Kiaora' is because he
liked orange juice.

(Did you notice? My sister Suki's name is sort of
Mum's names squashed together into a horrible

new one. I was lucky. 'Peter Ian' sounds kind of normal after that. Good job I'm not called 'Pixora' or something.)

Anyway, Bob said we should still do the party.

Mum was really upset, I could tell. But we all stomped down to the Osman Burger Bar and Kebab House, carrying twenty red balloons and not talking to each other.

Suki stayed behind to look after the Vampire Baby and Harry. It was daytime, so they were both fast asleep.

It was going to be the suckiest party ever. It was going to suck worse than a vampire with no teeth.

The party

Except that it wasn't sucky at all. It was awesome!

I had great presents. Tiffany bought me

chocolate. She also brought me a cork, which
Mum thought was funny – but she wouldn't say
why. The only word I thought she said was
'fart'.

Raj gave me a proper wooden baseball bat. Bob
gave me a tenner!

Dean Gosnall gave me a football shirt he didn't
want because it wasn't his team – but it was
new and everything.

Sky Taylor bought me this weird feathery thing
called a dreamcatcher. Mum said:

> 'All it will catch in our house will be dust
> and a few flies!'

I got so much stuff! We ate loads of burgers and chips and drank coke (not the proper stuff, but still good).

Then Bob got us all playing games. He just happened to have loads of things in a carrier bag he had just happened to bring with him. (just in case).

Game 1

We had to dress up in a Darth Vader mask, a hat and mittens and try to eat bits of chocolate with a knife and fork.

Raj was really good at it. He ate half a bar while we were laughing at Darth Vader with a Sikh handkerchief thing on his head.

Game 2

Bob got us into two teams. We had to pass a balloon from the front person to the back person without using our hands or arms.

Again Raj was easily the best. Does he have a Secret Life I don't Know about?

Game 3

We were in pairs and one of us had to make the other one into a zombie using a toilet roll.

It must have cost Bob loads, because there were about twenty of us and each pair had a toilet roll.

I thought:

'Maybe Bob has a special problem and has loads and loads of toilet rolls at home.'

Mum said:

'It's a waste. Bob should think of the children in Africa.'

Tiffany said:

'Why do they need OUR toilet rolls, Mrs Green? Don't they have supermarkets, Mrs Green?'

and:

'Do you have any pink paper, Mrs Green? I want to be a pink zombie!'

Mum said to Bob, very quietly:

    'If she was any dumber, she'd need

    watering.'

Tiffany's so cute! I still love her! I love her
even more now I don't have to talk to her very
much.

Then we all mucked about being zombies, until
it got hot in the toilet roll.

The cake

Of course there was no cake. But this didn't
faze SuperBob! He went out to the paper shop
and bought all the ice-creams it had.

44

He put them all into a big bowl and brought it in. There were all colours, and Magnums, and ice lollies ... all mashed up in this huge bowl with candles stuck in it.

Then they all sang 'Happy Birthday' and I blew out the candles.

I didn't cry – it was just some smoke from the candles got in my eyes.

Then everyone got a spoon and we all sort of pushed each other out of the way to eat the ice-cream cake. People at the front passed spoonfuls to the back and everyone was laughing and shouting and Gary Bracenose said to me:

'Your dad is awesome!'

and I didn't say anything for a moment. Then I said:

'Yes, he is!'

My mum smiled. (She looked a bit sad at the same time. It's a thing she does. It's weird, but you get used to it.)

46

Afterwards

So Mum said:

    'Say thank you to Bob!'

and I said:

    'Thank you to SuperBob,'

and he said:

    'That's OK. See you tomorrow, Susan!'

and I said,

    'Her name's not ... '

and Mum said:

    'Shut up, Pig!' and put her hand over my
    mouth, quite hard.

The donkey

We went home. Raj came with us because he was sleeping over. His whole family had gone down to London to see one of his zillions of aunts get engaged or married or buried or something.

Actually it wasn't a sleepover. It was a lying-awake-over. Nobody sleeps in our house, what with the Vampire Baby yelling and the hamster wheel squeaking away in the kitchen.

I was dead sure Dad would be sitting at the kitchen table waiting for us to come home. I ran up the garden path.

In the middle of the kitchen table was a big
straw donkey. It had a label on it that said:

    Sorry I couldn't make it, Pig, but I posted

    this from Spain. Something came up! Have

    a great birthday! Love you! Dad.

Mum made a funny snorting noise.

Raj said:

    'It's just not fair!'

Then Mum said:

'Give me the baseball bat, Rajesh!'

She swung it round her head a couple of times.

'Go on!' I yelled. 'Go on!'

She took a mighty swing and the donkey went flying across the kitchen. Wallop! Suki drop-kicked it to Raj, who was really angry for some reason. He hit it with a frying pan. Bong!

Mum was still whirling the bat and when she hit it again, the head flew off and straw rained down on us. We all started to laugh and we just couldn't stop.

Mum hugged me close.

'Happy unbirthday, Pig!' she said.

I was very happy. I was spending my first-ever unbirthday with my best-ever friends.

I said to Mum:

'Perhaps Dad missed the plane.'

She said:

'Perhaps, Pig. Perhaps.'

The next **PIG** book is

PIG

Skives off School

About the author

Barbara Catchpole was a teacher for thirty years and enjoyed every minute. She has three sons of her own who were always perfectly behaved and never gave her a second of worry.

Barbara also tells lies.